CUP FI

...wood **Primary School**
Gorsewood Road
Murdishaw
Runcorn
WA7 6ES
01928 712100

By Rob Ch

Illustrations by Elia Okstad

CONTENTS

CUP FINAL

It's Cup Final Day! St Patrick's Primary School and Oakfield Juniors – better known as the Saints and the Reds – have each won their way through the earlier rounds of the District Trophy to meet in the Final.

It's also March 17th, which just happens to be St Patrick's Day! The Saints are naturally hoping that this date will prove to be a good omen, but the Reds are determined to make it third time lucky against their local rivals. The Saints have already beaten them twice in the league.

Take a look at the teams and perhaps even choose which school you might like to support. Then read the stories and find out which team won the cup…

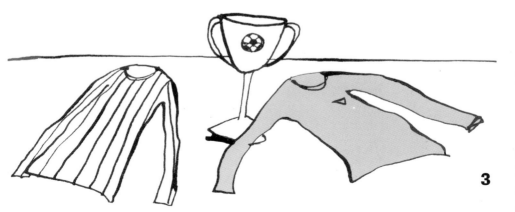

Oakfield Junior School

Headteacher: *Mr Fredericks*

Captain: *Connor*

Colours: *all red kit*

Nickname: *The Reds*

Team: *4-3-3 formation*

1
Jack

2
Ben

5
Sam

6
Chris

3
Afzal

4
Mohammed

8
Eddie

10
Dinesh

7
Liam

9
Connor

11
Sparrow

Substitutes:

12
Olivia

13
Surjit

14
Ryan

Captain's Notes:

Afraid we didn't do very well in the league this season. Finished next to bottom of the table and just avoided getting relegated. We let in too many goals, that was the trouble, but no disrespect to Jack who's our number one keeper. I ended up the team's top scorer, netting just one more than Sparrow. We've played our best football in the cup for some reason, winning all three games to reach the Final.

St Patrick's Primary School

Sports teacher: *Mr Scott*

Captain: *Bradley*

Colours: *green & white striped shirts, white shorts, green socks*

Nickname: *The Saints*

Team: *4-2-4 formation*

1
Lewis

2
Zoe

4
Nathan

5
Thomas

3
Matthew

8
Bradley

6
Ravi

7
Megan

9
Harry

10
Alex

11
William

Substitutes:

12
Jacob

13
Luke

14
Tyler

Captain's Notes:

Came runners-up in the league, but reckon we would've been Champions if we'd had a settled side. Perhaps tried too many different players and formations. Harry's the leading scorer for both the school and Oakfield Rangers – the Sunday League team that many of us Saints play for as well. We must be favourites for the District Trophy after doing the double over the Reds in the league this season.

Send on the Sub

(Oakfield Junior School)

"Good stop, Ollie!"

"Well saved!"

"You'll have Jack worried you might take his place in goal."

I laugh, because that comment was a joke, but the next one isn't very funny.

"You should've held on to the ball," Connor sneers at me. "They nearly scored from the rebound."

I have to bite my lip. If it had been anybody else but Connor, I might well have said something back. I mean, he *is* the school team captain. And Jack's his best mate.

It's a good job old Freddie doesn't let Connor pick the team or I'd never get a game. That's Mr Fredericks, by the way, our headteacher, who's taking us for this footie practice in the playground.

Even so, I've only played a couple of times this season for Oakfield Juniors. Pity we lost both matches, but still. It's not as though we've done all that great with Jack in goal. That's why we nearly got relegated – too many heavy defeats.

There's a saying in football – all goalies are crazy – and I reckon Jack must be, anyway. He throws himself around on the playground as if he's playing on grass. No wonder he's always getting cuts and grazes. You won't catch me doing dives on this surface. I like to think I'm not quite that crazy!

Besides, it really messes up your clothes. Mum goes mad if I come home with torn jeans.

"I do wish you'd play netball instead, Olivia," she often complains.

Bet Connor wishes that too!

It's true that I can catch and throw a ball better than I kick the thing, but I just love playing in goal. Dad tells me that, in his day, goalies didn't have to kick as much as we do nowadays. They were allowed to pick the ball up from back-passes and everything. Wish it was still like that. I'd be OK then.

Anyway, I'm rambling. Pre-match nerves, perhaps. We're playing in the Final of the District Trophy on Saturday against our local rivals, St Patrick's. Freddie's going to tell us the team selection after this practice. Just hope I might be named as one of the subs...

"Oi! Wake up, Ollie! They're attacking again."

"More like Dolly, I reckon – Dolly Day-Dream!"

"Yeah, keep your mind on the game, Dolly!"

Huh! Just listen to them. That's exactly what I *am* doing – on the Big Game.

★ ★ ★

Made it! Here I am on the subs' bench. Well, the park swings, anyway. Vandals have smashed the benches and I don't fancy plonking myself down on the grass. It's sopping wet after all the rain. Not so good for goalkeeping, not when the ball's skidding about like it is this morning.

The Saints' keeper would back me up on that, I'm sure. He had a shot from Connor a bit too well covered. The ball suddenly picked up speed off the grass, flew through his hands and smacked him right on the nose. The game had to be paused so their teacher could clean the blood off his face. The kid still wanted to

carry on, though. Guess he must be crazy too.

That's why you need a sub goalie – just in case the number one choice really *has* to come off. Mind you, it would have to be something pretty serious – like losing an arm or a leg.

Not that I want anything like that to happen to Jack, you understand. Well, not before half-time, anyway. But I'd love to get on the pitch at some point. Don't really want a medal just for sitting on a swing.

Best thing might be if we went, say, five goals up and Freddie could send on all the subs to let us join in the fun.

But it won't be one-sided like that of course – at least not in our favour. The Saints were runners-up in the league and we finished second to bottom. They beat us home and away, including a 4–1 defeat on our own ground a few weeks back.

Well, I say our own ground. There's just the playground at the school itself so we play our 'home' games on the local recreation ground.

Trouble is, the recky's used by everybody – and their dogs! Before kick-off, we have to go right over the pitch checking that all their *stuff* has been cleared up. Not very pleasant landing on top of a pile of smelly dog-poo.

This Cup Final is being played at the park where Oakfield Rangers also play their matches. Rangers are a Sunday League team which Connor and Jack play for, as well as some of the Saints mob. Must feel rather strange for them, playing against their Sunday teammates.

Whoops! Jack's just made a mess of things at a corner. He seemed to have the ball in his hands and then dropped it right at the feet of the Saints' number nine. All the kid had to do was poke it over the line.

That's 1–0 to them now and it looks like Jack's having to take some stick. Even Connor's not best pleased with him. Bet he'd have gone totally bananas, if it'd been *me* in goal.

Think I'll go and stand near Freddie for a bit – just to remind him I'm here. You never know, he might decide to make an early substitution…

Huh! Some hope of that. Jack's still in goal of course and he made a wicked save just before half-time to keep the score at one each.

Yeah, that's right. We're level again and so I'm back on the swing for the second half. Don't think there's much danger of me getting my gloves dirty today. I've taken them off and put them in my bag. Shame!

Great goal it was, by Sparrow. That's Alice Bird, by the way, the only other girl in our squad. Can't say she's a pal of mine – Sparrow's a bit of a loner – but it's nice to have her around so it's not just me. Y'know what I mean? The boys have to respect her. She's second top scorer behind Connor.

You can see why, too, with a goal like that. Saints have got a couple of girls in their team as well and Sparrow just left one of them for dead with her speed. Then she nutmegged their big centre-back, dodged past the keeper and smacked the ball into the net. She made them all look pretty silly.

So there we are. You're up to date now and it's... hang on, this looks promising. Sparrow's just zipped past the Saints' right back again – that poor girl's having a nightmare game – and…

"GOAL!"

Sorry – didn't mean to scream like that. Even fell off the swing in my excitement! We're 2–1 in front!

Connor couldn't miss. Sparrow plonked the ball right on his head and he's given her a great big hug. Amazing! Never thought I'd ever see him do anything like that!

Just going back to the touchline again to cheer the team on from there.

★ ★ ★

"C'mon, Ollie!" cries Sparrow. "Get those gloves on quick!"

I'm trying...I'm trying! Have you noticed how stupid gloves can be when you need to get the things on fast? You keep putting your fingers in all the wrong holes.

My big chance has suddenly come right out of the blue. Saints have been given a penalty and Jack's not fit enough to face it! He's gone and injured himself bringing their player down in the box.

"Connor's wanting to go in goal."

Sparrow's warning has made me panic even more. I can hear some of the parents calling for Connor too. Typical! Shows how much faith they've got in me.

Phew! Freddie's just waved me on. No time to be nervous. Must look confident – even if I don't feel it.

"Good luck, Olivia," Freddie says, forcing a smile. "Just do your best."

That's all I can do. I mean, nobody really expects a goalie to save a penalty, do they?

"Up to you now, Ollie," Jack mutters as Freddie

helps him off the pitch. He must be in a lot of pain, the way he's holding his arm across his chest, but he's trying hard not to show it. "Don't let them equalize."

I nod but this is no time for a chat. I know what he means. The Saints don't deserve to draw level. There's only been one team in it this half and we should've won the match by now. Even Connor and Sparrow have missed easy chances to score.

I shake my head to try and clear it. All that matters now is what's about to happen. Like Jack said: *it's up to me.*

I can almost feel every pair of eyes drilling into me. I get into position right in the centre of the goal and realise how big the space is around me – and how small I am.

For some reason, I remember once being inside a huge silent church on my own. I couldn't resist shouting out and listening to the echoes bounce off the stone walls.

I have to stop myself doing the same thing now. There's an eerie hush about the place, just like in that church. Only Sparrow's voice manages to get through to me.

"You can do it, Ollie," I hear her cry.

I glance up but can't pick her out. The players are all stretched out along the edge of the penalty area, waiting and watching. They look just like a row of coloured shirts on the washing line – the reds mixed up with the green and white stripes.

Time has almost stopped. Everything seems to be happening in slow motion...

The kicker - their ginger-haired captain - is fiddling with the ball, trying to place it just right...

I stare at the trademark on the ball and the dirt on one of the letters...

The boy stands up and starts to take some steps backwards...

I bounce up and down on the line to relax my tensed muscles...

...slap my gloves together...

...then flap my arms about as if I'm trying to take off...

Peeeeppppp!!!

The referee's blast on the whistle breaks the spell.

Time speeds up and the boy runs towards me. I still don't know which way to dive. Instinct takes over. He kicks the ball and I throw myself to the right. I don't even see the ball coming. It's a blur. But I feel it. Smacks me on the leg as I hit the ground.

Where's it gone? Got no idea.

All I know for sure is that the ball's not in the net.

Noise bursts out all around me – from the players, from the spectators. Sparrow's the first to reach me and yells into my ear.

"Magic, Ollie! What a star!"

More teammates pile on top of us and we sink into the goalmouth mud under the weight of all the bodies. I can hardly breathe. It takes the referee ages to break up the scrum and rescue me.

Even Connor slaps me on the back, almost knocking me over again. "Couldn't have done any better myself, Ollie," he admits with a grin. "You've just gone and won us the Cup!"

He was right too. And here's the medal in my hand to prove it. First thing I've ever won in sport and it feels good!

Bet I'll have another reminder of the game – a bruise on my leg where the ball struck me!

The final score was 3–1, by the way. The Saints seemed to give up after they missed that penalty and we grabbed another goal just before the end.

"You deserve that medal," Dad told me. "The Saints might have gone on to win if they'd made it two each."

"We're really proud of you," Mum smiled, putting her arm around me. "We'll have to come and cheer you on next season."

Yes, my parents were there! They turned up at half-time and I didn't even know till afterwards. Perhaps it's as well they saw what happened or they might never have believed me.

Just hope you do…

Bird on the Wing

(Oakfield Junior School)

"Out to me! Wing it!"

Sparrow's shouts went unheard – or perhaps unheeded. The ball was booted into the penalty area instead and headed away to safety.

"See!" cried Sparrow. "Give it to me next time."

The Reds' number eleven stamped the ground in frustration. It was the only thing the winger *had* kicked so far, apart from having a sly flick at a defender's leg when the referee was looking the other way.

Sparrow stood near the touchline, arms outstretched like a scarecrow in baggy clothes. The all-red kit was faded and shapeless after many seasons of washing – and at least two sizes too big.

"I've hardly had a touch of the ball yet," Sparrow complained. "I'm freezing."

"Well get involved in the game, then," Connor snapped. "Don't just stand there waiting for the ball to come to you."

Sparrow pulled a face as the captain ran back to help in defence. "Huh! No wonder we're losing. There's only me left up in attack half the time."

The Reds of Oakfield Juniors had made a bad start to the Cup Final. An error by Jack in goal allowed their local rivals, St Patrick's Primary School, to take the lead and the Saints were now right on top. A second goal seemed to be more a matter of *when* it would come, not *if* it might.

As the shivering Sparrow watched the action from afar, it looked like that moment had arrived. The ball was played into the Reds' penalty area, straight to the feet of the Saints' goal scorer.

Harry, full of confidence after that early success, saw the chance to strike again. He steadied himself, took careful aim and steered his shot wide of the goalkeeper.

Not wide enough. Jack hurled himself to his left and just managed to get his hand to the ball. He deflected it past the post for a corner kick.

"Great save!" yelled Connor. "That makes up for the other one."

The Saints nearly scored again, though, from the corner. As the ball curled into the goalmouth, the Saints' centre-back jumped higher than anyone else but put his header over the crossbar.

The Oakfield Juniors headteacher, Mr Fredericks, gave a sigh of relief. "This is going to be a cricket score, if we don't pull our socks up," he muttered.

He didn't like calling out from the touchline. He felt it was a little undignified if the players' parents heard him ranting and raving. Besides, he knew he could leave it to the parents themselves to do that sort of thing.

"Sort it out, Reds!" shouted one mother nearby.

"Show 'em what you're made of!" cried her husband.

"Get stuck in!" demanded another father. "They're all over us like a rash!"

Mr Fredericks didn't really approve of such comments, but felt he couldn't do much to stop them. It often seemed to him that the parents wanted the team to win even more than their own children did.

"Just hope we can hold out till half-time," he murmured. "Might be able to change a few things then – perhaps put on a couple of subs..."

The headteacher's thoughts were interrupted by yet another attack on his team's goal. He watched helplessly as the Saints' ginger-haired captain fired a powerful shot from the edge of the penalty area.

Jack didn't even make a move. The ball whistled over the keeper's head and cracked against the wooden crossbar like a thunderclap.

The rebound cleared everyone inside the area and dropped to Connor who controlled the ball with a single touch. Without even looking up, he hooked it away towards the left wing, knowing that a certain player would still be lurking there.

He was right too.

Sparrow, however, was not on her own. Zoe, the Saints' right-back, and Nathan, the big central defender, were keeping an eye on her. The Saints knew how dangerous Sparrow could be, if given too much space. Although they had beaten the Reds twice in the league, Sparrow had scored in both matches.

Sparrow remembered that fact, too, and was keen to find the back of their net again. She was quicker off the mark than Zoe and reached the ball first. Sparrow screened it skilfully with her body then turned so suddenly that Zoe lost her balance and slipped.

Leaving a miserable Zoe sitting uncomfortably in a puddle of water, Sparrow skipped along the touchline, drawing the other defender towards her like a moth to a flame.

Nathan knew better, though, than to dive in with a tackle too soon. He had already learnt, to his cost, that Sparrow's fast feet could make any defender feel foolish.

He hoped to delay Sparrow's progress long enough for extra help to arrive, but his plan didn't work. The winger's burst of speed took him by surprise. Nathan had expected her to dribble her way down the touchline, but Sparrow ran straight at him instead and pushed the ball between his long thin legs.

In desperation, he tried to grab her flapping shirt as she darted past, but he wasn't even quick enough to foul her. Sparrow was away, sprinting towards goal with only the keeper now to beat. Lewis never stood a chance.

She loved one-on-one situations like this. Very rarely did any goalkeeper come out on top in such a personal duel. Sparrow's trickery was too much for them.

As the boy came off his line to meet her, Sparrow shaped to take the ball to his left before spinning the other way instead. Lewis was completely wrong-footed. He dived down into the mud in vain while Sparrow enjoyed the luxury of drilling the ball into the empty net to level the scores at 1–1.

She ran off in delight to do her usual little jig of celebration around one of the corner flags. It was a solo performance until several teammates finally arrived on the scene, dancing and jumping all over each other.

The referee was not best pleased. "Right, that's enough, Reds," he called out. "Break up the party. Let's get on with the game."

The Saints could hardly believe what had happened.

"No way she should have got past both of you," the captain moaned at Nathan and Zoe. "That was dead sloppy defending."

Zoe hung her head, not wanting to meet Bradley's glare, but Nathan was more prepared to answer back.

"Don't blame us, Brad," he retorted. "That Sparrow kid's wicked. Bet you couldn't have stopped her either."

Bradley pulled a face and then turned away to rally his team. "C'mon, Saints, concentrate," he cried out, rolling up his sleeves. "We know we can beat this lot."

The shock equalizer, however, changed the pattern of play. The game became much more of an equal contest for the rest of the first half, with both goalkeepers kept on their toes. Lewis did well to block shots from Connor and Sparrow, while Jack pulled off another superb save just before half-time.

"Well done, Jack!" Mr Fredericks praised him as the players gathered around the headteacher for a much needed breather. "And well done, everybody. You've played some good football after a shaky start."

The headteacher made a point of singling out Sparrow, too, for a special mention.

"That was a very well-taken goal, Alice," he told her. "Not many people have the skills to beat opponents and keep a cool head in situations like that."

Sparrow felt embarrassed. She knew what some of the others might be thinking. In front of goal was about the only place that she did manage to remain calm.

In school, it was often a different matter. Sparrow had a temper as quick as her feet. Only yesterday she had been involved in a lunchtime spat with Dinesh, who played behind her in midfield for the Reds.

Fortunately, Connor had stepped between them before the teacher on duty had noticed.

"What's the matter with you two?" Connor demanded. "You want to get banned from the Final or something?"

"She started it," Dinesh claimed.

"Right – and I'll finish it," said the captain as Sparrow gave a shrug. "Keep out of each other's way till the bell goes. Got it?"

They got his message loud and clear. Neither of them was foolish enough to want to tangle with Connor. They were still not on speaking terms, however, and Dinesh had made no effort to congratulate Sparrow on her goal.

Mr Fredericks ended his half-time pep talk with words of encouragement for the players.

"Keep this up now," he urged. "Play as a team and you can win this match. Good luck!"

As the group broke up, Connor pulled Sparrow and Dinesh together. "Talking of playing as a team," he hissed, "don't think I haven't noticed that you two ain't even passed the ball to each other yet."

Sparrow tugged her sleeve out of his grip. "So what's new?" she said with a scowl. "Nobody passes to me, anyway."

"Rubbish!" Connor retorted. "How come you score so many goals?"

"No thanks to him," she muttered. "He's useless. Don't know why old Freddie keeps picking him."

"Same reason he keeps picking you."

"Oh yeah – and what's that?"

The captain looked her in the eye. "'Cos Dinny's worth his place in the team, that's why – just like you."

Sparrow had no answer to that. It was the nearest Connor had ever actually come to praising her. She wandered away to her position on the left wing to wait for the match to restart, thinking about what he'd just said.

Being in the school team was important to her. Playing football was one of the few things she was really good at, and she could still remember the thrill of seeing her own name on the teamsheet for the first time.

11 – A. Bird

As Sparrow had stood gazing at the sports noticeboard, two boys came up behind her.

"Hey! Look!" cackled one of them. "There's a bird on the wing!"

"Yeah," sneered the other. "A little *black*-bird!"

For once, Sparrow didn't react to the taunts. She'd grown used to people making fun of her name and even her colour sometimes too. Nothing could spoil that special moment. She was in the team – and that was all that mattered.

The referee's whistle jerked her mind back to the present. As the Reds launched an early attack, Sparrow sprinted forward in support.

"Yes – to me!" she cried. "I'm free."

When Dinesh responded to her demand, Sparrow was so surprised to receive a pass from him that she let the ball slide under her boot and out of play. Dinesh smirked and Connor glared, neither needing to say anything.

A few minutes later, Sparrow made amends for her mistake. Brushing past Zoe, she glanced up and picked out her target – Connor's head. Her cross to the far post was perfect. The ball curled over Nathan's leap and landed smack on the striker's forehead.

As the ball rocketed past Lewis into the top corner of the net, Connor wheeled away in delight towards Sparrow, a wide grin spreading across his face.

The captain lifted the winger off her feet in a bear hug, almost squeezing the breath from her thin body.

"You little beauty!" he cried, before dropping her to the ground in a heap as other team-mates caught up with them.

Sparrow crawled from the crush. "Phew!" she gasped. "Think that must mean I've been forgiven!"

The Reds now enjoyed their best spell of the match, keeping the Saints' defence very busy. They should have increased their narrow 2–1 lead on several occasions, but a combination of bad luck and bad shooting let them down.

Dinesh, for example, hit the side netting when it seemed easy to score and Sparrow somehow scooped the ball over the bar from close range. Even Connor was guilty of a terrible miskick, his wild slice nearly sending the ball into orbit.

Mr Fredericks paced the touchline. "We might live to regret all these misses," he muttered. "I can feel it in my bones."

His aching bones soon appeared to be correct. The Saints broke away on a rare attack and Harry's long run towards goal was only brought to a halt by Jack's reckless lunge.

Their collision left both boys winded and wounded. The injury to Jack's right arm, however, was more serious than Harry's gashed knee and the goalkeeper was in no fit state to carry on.

It was only as Mr Fredericks decided he would have to use his substitute keeper that he realised something else. Saints had been awarded a penalty!

"Foul by the goalie inside the area," announced the referee.

"C'mon, Ollie – get those gloves on quick," Sparrow shouted towards the touchline where the reserve goalkeeper was preparing for action.

Mr Fredericks waved the substitute onto the pitch.

"Good luck, Olivia," he said simply. "Just do your best."

"Up to you now, Ollie," added Jack as he was led away, arm across his chest in pain. "Don't let them equalize."

She smiled nervously and went to take up her position on the goal-line.

"You can do it, Ollie," Sparrow cried, to try to boost the keeper's confidence.

"She'd better," Connor muttered.

Bradley, the Saints' captain, placed the ball on the muddy penalty spot and took several paces back. He hoped that he looked more confident than he felt. The limping Harry was his side's usual penalty-taker.

The whistle blew and Olivia bounced up and down on the line as Bradley ran towards her. Both players' eyes were fixed on the ball rather than each other and as the kicker made contact, the goalie dived to her right.

Olivia failed to get her gloved hands anywhere near the ball. It smacked against her legs instead and looped up and over the bar.

"She's saved it!" whooped Sparrow, dodging past the kneeling Bradley to haul the goalkeeper back onto her feet. "Magic, Ollie! What a star!"

There was little doubt as to which team was going to win the match now. The penalty miss seemed to deflate the Saints' spirits like a leaking balloon. The Reds, by contrast, were inspired and added a third goal just before the end to clinch their 3–1 victory. It was a shock, however, to see who was allowed to score it.

With the goal at her mercy, Sparrow slid the ball sideways into the path of Dinesh. Taken by surprise, he scuffed his shot but the ball trickled over the line before the goalkeeper could scramble across to smother it.

"Thanks, Sparrow," Dinesh said bashfully.

"Just so that Connor can't accuse me of never passing to you," she replied, holding out her hand.

As Dinesh took it, Sparrow dug her fingernails into his flesh to make him wince.

"Just don't expect me to do it again," she said with an impish grin.

Put on the Spot

(St Patrick's – The Saints)

*Fancy playing the District
Trophy Final on St Patrick's
Day! Got to be a lucky day
for us Saints, surely. It's even
stopped raining at last now
we're out on the pitch – still
a strong wind, though. Just
hope I win the toss…*

"Heads!"

The spinning coin
plopped into a puddle in
the centre-circle and three pairs of eyes peered
down at the queen's mud-splattered face.

"Huh! That's the only thing you'll win this
morning, Ginger," grunted Connor, the opposing

captain. "The Cup's ours."

Bradley grinned. Connor only
called him Ginger when he
was annoyed. "No chance. It's
St Patrick's Day, remember."

The referee wiped the dirty coin on his sleeve. "So what are you going to do, Saints?" he demanded.

"Change ends," Bradley told him. "We'll have the wind behind us first half."

The referee signalled the decision to the teams and then placed the match ball with a squelch onto the freshly painted centre spot. "Right, your kick off, Reds."

The captains shook hands briefly as they crossed over. They were team-mates for their Sunday League side, Oakfield Rangers, but their friendship was now put on hold for the next hour. School pride was at stake in this Cup Final and both boys wanted to be the victorious skipper holding the trophy aloft after the match.

"Best of luck," Bradley said with a smile.

"You don't mean that, Ginger," Connor retorted.

"No, I don't. We're gonna thrash you lot!"

We'd better do. Already beat Connor's mob twice in the league so we should be OK. Just got to keep a watch on that Sparrow on the wing. She's their real danger man - well, girl, anyway...

★ ★ ★

The green-striped shirts of St Patrick's Primary School seemed to outnumber the reds of Oakfield Juniors, so much were the Saints on top in the opening minutes of the game.

"C'mon, big effort, Saints," Bradley demanded loudly. "We want an early goal."

His players responded with one attack after another, hardly allowing the Reds to get the ball over the halfway line. The one time they managed to do so, Connor's low shot zipped off the wet grass and struck the Saints' goalkeeper in the face. It gave him a bloody nose and everyone else took a breather while Lewis received some treatment.

It wasn't very long, though, before play switched back to the other end of the pitch. An awkward shot from Bradley forced the Reds' keeper, Jack, to dive full-length to deflect the ball around the post for a corner.

It was clear which of the two goalkeepers had seen more of the action. Lewis may well have had some bloodstains on his top, but there were black muddy streaks all down the front and sides of Jack's yellow outfit.

"You look like a giant bumblebee!" cackled Connor, slapping his mate on the back.

Their grins didn't last very long. The wind swirled the corner into the goalmouth, but most of the time Jack would have gathered the ball comfortably. Sadly, this time he didn't. He spoiled his previous good work by letting the ball slip through his grasp and the Saints' leading scorer tapped it into the unguarded net.

"Cheers, Jack!" Harry mocked. "Very generous of you!"

Before Jack could reply, Harry was surrounded by the celebrating Saints and swept away towards the halfway line.

We deserved that. Doesn't matter how they go in. They all count. And Harry's keeping count. He reckons that's his twentieth goal of the season. And he should know – he's always top in Maths...

Harry's twenty-first goal was almost notched up a few minutes later. His shot was on its way to the goal until Jack made a great save with his fingertips.

Now it was Jack's turn to gloat. "Sorry, pal. Can't let you score again."

Harry shrugged. "Plenty of time."

He was right about that too. The game was only ten minutes old.

The Saints came close to adding a second goal, in fact, from the corner that followed. Nathan, their lanky centre-back, used his extra height well, rising above everybody to meet the ball with a powerful header. He just saw it skim the crossbar before he landed and toppled over into the mud.

"Unlucky!" Bradley consoled him as he helped a winded Nathan back onto his feet. "C'mon, Saints, keep this up – we've got 'em on the run!"

Another goal now will kill 'em off. They've already got their parents on their backs, screaming at 'em from the touchline. Hate that kind of thing. Glad Dad always keeps his mouth shut, even if we're playing like dummies. He knows we're trying our best.

Good – got the ball back again – we could be in here...

"Great tackle, Matt!" shouted Bradley. "Play it up the wing."

The Saints' full-back did exactly that. Matthew pushed the ball along the left touchline for the winger to take in his stride. William, the number eleven, looked up to see that their captain had also joined the attack and then slid the ball into Bradley's path just outside the penalty area.

The invitation to shoot was too tempting to refuse. Bradley needed one touch to tee the ball up and his next was a really hard strike at goal. It was doubtful whether Jack even saw the ball until it bounced back over his head from the vibrating crossbar.

Can't believe that didn't go in. Not my day today – that's two goals I could've had already. And now they're on the attack instead. That Sparrow's got the ball. Better try and get back to help out…

"Hold her off! Don't let her run at you!"

Bradley was wasting his breath. Sparrow in full flight took some stopping. Zoe, her main marker, and Nathan failed in their attempts to halt her and so did the Saints' goalkeeper.

Lewis had raced out to meet Sparrow and dived down at her feet, but the ball was no longer there. Lewis knew where it was though. He'd heard the ripple of the netting as he sprawled on the ground. He could also hear the captain complaining.

"That was dead sloppy defending."

"Don't blame us, Brad," Nathan replied. "That Sparrow kid's wicked. Bet you couldn't have stopped her either."

Bradley pulled a face, suspecting that Nathan was probably right. "C'mon, Saints, concentrate," he urged his team, rolling up his sleeves in a determined manner. "We know we can beat this lot."

St Patrick's sports teacher, Mr Scott, called out from the touchline in support of his captain. "That's the way, Bradley. Drive them forward. Let's have another goal."

Huh! Easier said than done, Scotty. That goal's bound to fire 'em up, catching us on the break like that. There's Connor now, going round and shaking his fists at all of 'em. He'll make sure they've got the message OK. Well, I've just got to do the same. That's the skipper's job – lead by example...

As Bradley feared, that equalizer had boosted the Reds' confidence. They might have taken the lead if Lewis hadn't stopped both Sparrow and Connor with brave blocks. It was a good job that Jack remained alert at the other end. Only a fine save from him, just before half-time, kept the scores level at 1–1.

When the whistle went for the break, Bradley trudged towards Mr Scott who had come onto the pitch in his wellies to talk to the players. The captain stood brooding on the edge of the group, taking occasional swigs from a water bottle and not really listening to the teacher.

If only my shot had gone in... we'd have been two up then and they'd never have scored like they did. Stupid goal to go and give away. Don't reckon Zoe's up to it – knew Scotty shouldn't have picked her in the first place...

"So what do you think, captain?"

Bradley's head jerked up. He had no idea what Mr Scott was asking him about. He reddened a bit as other eyes turned his way and he saw Nathan smirking.

"Er…um," he began, if only to break the lengthening silence. "Er…I think we're giving that little winger too much space and…"

"Yes, I've already dealt with that, Bradley," the teacher interrupted him. "Zoe knows what she has to do in the second half."

Bradley took a deep breath and decided to speak his mind. "Well, I just think we ought to bring Tyler on, y'know, in Zoe's place, like…"

He stalled for a moment, realising that Zoe was glaring at him, then went on, "I mean, Tyler's quick and a good tackler. Nobody can dribble past him easily."

Mr Scott nodded. "That's why Tyler's in the squad," he said, knowing that the two boys were good friends. "But you seem to forget that even Tyler couldn't stop that girl scoring in the recent league game. Zoe deserves a chance here to show what she can do."

"Yeah, nothing," Bradley muttered under his breath, taking another gulp of water to try and hide his annoyance.

"What I was actually asking you," the teacher continued, "as team captain, was whether you think we should switch to a 4-3-3 system like theirs? We seem to be getting rather over-run in midfield."

Bradley realised that Mr Scott knew he hadn't been paying attention. "Might be worth a try," he agreed with a shrug.

"Right, we'll do that, then," said Mr Scott. "But just remember that you can't be everywhere, Bradley. Hold your own position a bit more this half."

As the teacher explained the new formation he wanted them to employ, Bradley scuffed at a clump of mud with his left boot to avoid any further eye contact with Nathan or anyone else. The captain wasn't used to being criticised in front of his team-mates and he didn't like it.

Huh! Scotty thinks he's such a great coach, always changing tactics and stuff. If we'd had a full-strength team every match, reckon we would have won the league. We dropped some dead stupid points 'cos of that sort of thing.

Right, c'mon, then – belt up, Scotty, and just let us get on with it...

The second half began disastrously for the Saints. Within minutes of the restart, Sparrow had ruined all their half-time plans.

Receiving the ball near the touchline, the winger's speed left Zoe a long way behind. Sparrow had time now to steady herself, look up and then plant her cross kick right on Connor's head.

The Saints' goalkeeper was left helpless. Lewis could only watch the ball fly past him into the top corner of the net.

Connor's goal celebrations knew no bounds. The Reds' captain danced across the penalty area, shrieking his delight, and yanked Sparrow off her feet in a rib-crushing hug.

"You little beauty!" he screamed to the heavens.

Bradley, by contrast, squatted on his haunches and spat on the ground in disgust.

"Brilliant!" he snorted sarcastically, staring across towards their downcast coach. "Good job Zoe knows what she has to do, Scotty, or we could *really* be in trouble…"

Over the next ten minutes or so, the subdued Saints were totally outplayed. Even Bradley was unable to raise his own game and demand that his team did likewise. They were very lucky not to find themselves falling further behind. Both Sparrow and Connor wasted golden opportunities to win the match for them, shooting high and wide when they had been well placed to score.

The belated substitution of Zoe did little to strengthen the Saints' defence. Her replacement, Tyler, also struggled against Sparrow but at least he could kick the ball harder – and further. When he hoofed a clearance upfield, it sent the unmarked Harry sprinting away towards the Reds' goal.

It was one against one – striker versus keeper – with Harry favourite to win the contest until he was flattened by Jack's clumsy challenge.

Penalty!

Phew! Thought for a minute the ref wasn't going to give it. Took him ages to point to the spot. Just listen to Connor moaning. It was Jack's own fault he got hurt. Think he might even have to go off – must be serious. That's bad news for Rangers too.

Wonder who'll go in goal now? Looks like Connor wants to – he's trying to get Jack's gloves off him. Just hope Harry's OK – don't like the way he's hobbling around. Better go and check...

"You OK?" asked Bradley.

Harry winced as he put the weight on his left leg. "Dunno," he grunted, bending to examine the cut on his knee. "It's a bit sore."

"Good job it's not your right leg."

"Yeah, but it's the one I stand on as I kick. Worried it might give way."

"But you always take the penalties."

Harry forced a grin. "Might have to leave this one to you."

"Me?"

"Yeah, well, you're captain. Who else is there?"

Bradley glanced around, almost in desperation. Nobody seemed keen to volunteer their services.

"William? Tyler?"

Harry pulled a face. "You've got to be joking. C'mon, Brad, I've seen you slam them past Lewis in practice."

"That's different. I've never taken one in a proper match before, not even for Rangers."

"Well you'll never have a better chance to score," Harry said, nodding towards the touchline. "Look who they're putting in goal."

A girl! That makes it even worse somehow. After what I said at half-time, bet Zoe would never let me live it down if I go and miss. Can't get out of it now. Scotty's pointing at me...

"Up to you now, Ollie," Jack told her as he was led off the pitch, holding his right arm across his chest in pain. "Don't let them equalize."

Olivia took up her position on the goal-line, but Bradley didn't even look at the new goalkeeper. He didn't want to catch her eye and perhaps show his own nervousness. He focused all his attention on the ball instead, bouncing it a few times in the mud before placing it carefully on the penalty spot.

This has just got to go in. GOT to!

If I score, we're back level and maybe give us the edge to go on and win the game. If I miss – well, don't even want to think about that…

Now, do I blast it or sidefoot it? Dunno – not sure. Harry usually relies on pure power. Guess I might as well do the same.

Just wish it wasn't so muddy – don't want to slip over and make myself look an idiot…

Right, stay calm, Brad, concentrate – here goes…

Cries of support rang out for both players then a hush descended over the pitch in anticipation of the duel.

The silence was broken by the referee's whistle and Bradley ran in, eyes fixed on the ball, ignoring the goalie's distracting antics on the line.

Wwhhaaack!!

His right boot made good firm contact, firing the ball almost dead straight at the middle of the goal. But Olivia was no longer there. She had hurled herself to one side, arms outstretched, and the ball crashed into her flailing legs.

Bradley watched the ball spiral upwards and then drop agonisingly over the crossbar onto the roof of the netting.

Bradley sank to his knees in despair as red-clad bodies rushed past him to mob their goalkeeper and whoop their relief.

Harry limped forward to console his captain. "Unlucky, Brad," he said, helping him to his feet. "Can't win 'em all."

Bradley wiped a muddy sleeve across his face, making sure that no stray tears would betray him. He'd save any crying for later, in the privacy of his own bedroom.

"Well, we won't win this one now, that's for sure," he murmured, his voice cracking. "Thanks to me."

"Don't go blaming yourself, Brad. Nobody else was brave enough to take it," Harry told him before confessing the truth. "And that includes me."

There was still enough time left in the match for another goal to be scored, in fact, but it made no real difference to the outcome.

The disappointed Saints offered little further defence and Sparrow took full advantage of poor marking. She could have scored herself but unselfishly set up a team-mate instead for a simple tap-in to make the final score 3–1 to the Reds.

It was all over.

Wish that were me up there now, receiving that cup. Just look at Connor, grinning his head off and waving the cup about like a maniac. Bet he's going to really love rubbing it in tomorrow at the Rangers' game by flashing his medal around. Still, guess I'd have probably done just the same in his boots.

Oh, well, like Harry said, you can't win 'em all. Thanks for nothing, St Patrick!

Roll on Easter. We've got the Sunday League Cup Final then. You never know, I might yet end the season with a winner's medal myself...

Glossary

do the double - beat a team both home and away
- or to win both the league and
cup tournaments

equalize - level the scores in a match

extra time - time added to end of cup game,
if scores are level, in order to try
and gain a result

formations - patterns or arrangements of
players on the pitch, for example,
4-2-4 means a team lines up with
four defenders, two players in
midfield and four attackers (note
that goalkeepers are not included)

interval - break of a few minutes in the
middle of a game, often known as
half-time

nutmeg - kick the ball through another
player's legs

penalty - foul punished by a direct kick at goal from the penalty spot with only the goalkeeper to beat

penalty box - rectangular area of the pitch in front of each goal

relegation - team or teams at the bottom of the league table being demoted to play in a lower division next season

runners-up - team finishing second in the league or cup

screening - shielding the ball away from the opponent with one's own body

substitution - when one player replaces another player during a game

subs' bench - place for substitutes to wait before going onto the pitch

touchline - painted white line marking the side of the pitch